By Any Other Circumstances

BY: KAREN PIVOTT

www.amazon.com/author/karenpivott

BY THE SAME AUTHOR

BOOKS ON KINDLE

NON FICTION

Airbags and Starting Over

Back On the Road Again

Always Travel With Your Basket

CHILDRENS FICTION

Birthdays at the Bay

Royce and Billy

FICTION

By Any Other Circumstances

4900 LaCross Road
North Charleston, SC 29406
USA

First Printing, Create Space 2016

ISBN-9780473274726

Published in New Zealand

FOREWORD

Jenna was one of those young women who let life carry her along, and she was carried for many years believing that she was right with her world, and that her world was right with the world. Jenna received a wake-up call and ever since then Jenna and her world began to change. Through all the changes though Jenna discovered herself and the importance family.

Disclaimer

This is a work of fiction. Names, characters, business, places, events and incidents are either the product of the author's imagination or used in a fictitious manner. Any resemblance to actual persons, living or dead, or actual events is purely coincidence.

KAREN PIVOTT

ACKNOWLEDGEMENT

With thanks and love always to my husband Alan.

Chapter 1.

The day started like any other.
Jenna rose, showered, dressed then made
her way to the kitchen. The glass of water
readied the night before was on the bench
as she had left it, covered with a small
piece of net. The two small white tablets
she had been taking for years were in the
small covered container next to the drink.
Jenna took the tablets from their
container and put them in her mouth,
then dutifully drank the water swallowed
the tablets and walked over to the
calendar on the wall to remind herself of
what she was expected to do this day the
2nd of June.

Breakfast was made, a glass of
cranberry juice was poured from the glass
jug in the fridge. The kettle was put on to
boil and coffee was measured into a mug.

And so the day was unfolding as

usual. The day that was organised, the day like all the others. Ordered. Simplistic. Predictable. Routine.

Routine was Jenna's life blood in these her, "twilight years" as the children would tease her. No surprises. No unexpected encounters of any kind was just how Jenna liked it. No more than that was needed.

Jenna the successful business woman. Jenna the loving grandmother. Nan to her grandchildren. Jenna the woman who had time for people as they needed her. Jenna who attended meetings across the month for various committees.

There was a time in her early twenties when Jenna found it difficult to fit going along to the Plunket committee meetings and the kindergarten steering group meetings, with her family commitments. Then there was the matter of Jenna herself fitting in. Jenna had always been a good, reliable worker in any endeavour, however her circumstances at that time meant she had gone from wealthy to hard up in literally three months flat. Jenna could never understand if her presence was tolerated or an embarrassment to the other women in the groups. Two of these women's husbands had been directly responsible for the demise Jenna and her family found themselves in. Money then no money, then more money, then less money. Jenna had decided when the money went the first time that instead of being upset about it she would be thankful there was plenty of room for more money to flow in and it had. Like the tide. Full tide and low tide.

"Stop dwelling on the past." Jenna chided herself and set about her day.

By all accounts today was a quiet one. A meeting with Reverend Nichols at 10.00 a.m., followed by lunch at 12.00 p.m. with her daughter in law Deanna to go over the surprise birthday plans for her twelve year old grandson, Richard, then home again. Once home it would be feet up and finish the latest Michael Connelly novel.

Jenna was indeed doing this when she heard a knock on the door. Putting her bookmark in the book then placing it on the round table Jenna rose and went to the front door.

A man with his back to her was standing there. On hearing her say "Good afternoon how may help you?" He turned and looked directly at her.

"I thought it must have been you. I read the article in the local paper about giving train rides to those who need a lift? You have lost a lot of weight it suits you." He displayed a whimsical smile.

Jenna stood transfixed.

"I know it's been awhile. Are you

going to ask me in? I could do with a coffee. I can make it if you point me in the right direction just like the old days."

"No I don't think so." Jenna heard herself say.

"Look about all that."

Jenna cut him off mid-sentence "I think you should leave. I can see you are well and haven't changed a bit."

With a raised eyebrow he turned and made his way down the steps to his car. He got into the car and waited as if Jenna was going to call him back or go after him, but after what seemed a long time he started his car and drove away down the tree lined driveway.

"How can I be standing here as he drives away feeling nothing?" Jenna said to the light breeze which had come from seemingly nowhere. Jenna walked around to the verandah and sat on the white timber chair.

The past had collided all be it briefly with her present, and Jenna was taken aback. This was the man that Jenna had loved, not as a lover, not as a brother, but loved just the same when she was married. How that had happened did itself cause confusion and concern for her, but it didn't make the feeling any less real. A tangible thing is love. The only explanation Jenna had then and now was that they met at a time of great change in their lives. A time when under any other set of circumstances they would never have met at all.

Jenna walked back inside and it wasn't until she went to fill the jug that Jenna realised she was shaking. Physically shaking. Holding the bench to steady herself she took a deep breath and looked out the window at her trees, grass, anything familiar, and when the shaking began to subside she walked over to her chair sat down and tried to make sense of the encounter. Why now? Was the first thought followed swiftly by that reception to stop any further visits, prearranged or not.

Jenna's thoughts were interrupted by the phone ringing. "Hello."

"Jenna. It's Reverend Nichols. Have I got the day wrong?"

"No. I'm so sorry time has got away on me. Shall we reschedule?"

"No just come when you're ready I'm not going anywhere."

Jenna felt embarrassed, missing appointments was not something Jenna did or had ever done. First time for everything she thought. Not feeling like going to the meeting at all Jenna picked up her belongings, and headed for the door reasoning that to be busy might be the very best thing. On arriving at the door Jenna promptly put her belongings down, and went back to the kitchen to check if she had put the jug on, finding the tap on and water running into an over full jug still sitting in the sink.

Chapter 2.

June 22

The days were starting to meld together. They were crisp days. The winter chill was in the air, but the rain was still a fair way off if the weather forecasts could be believed.

Jenna smiled to herself at this thought. For years her husband Adam had kept meticulous records of the weather in order to prove the meteorologists were wrong. In his later years this had become his passion. In his later years? That in itself was a contradiction. Adam had passed away at the age of fifty six years. Thirty two years and twelve days after their marriage. Jenna found herself a widow at the age of fifty.

Theirs had been an unconventional marriage according to many, however that did not deter Adam from his courting, then proposing, to the quiet seventeen year old. A first marriage for them both.

Jenna's parents seemed pleased someone would take their daughter off their hands.

Jenna was not one to go dating and that in itself created discussion amongst the small community.

Adam literally drove into town. Swept the town off its feet in no time at all but with Jenna, well that was a completely different matter.

Jenna was studying to go to University and oblivious to the overtures of Adam.

Their first meeting was at the library. Adam walked boldly up to Jenna and asked her if she would like a thick shake. Looking up from her book she said politely

"There is no eating or drinking in the Library the signs are everywhere."

"I was rather hoping we could go to the local tea shop to have them?"

"Not today I'm afraid". Jenna countered "I am taking solace in my reading."

"Solace?" Adam replied "A rather sombre word for one so young."

Jenna quite taken aback by his words and his tone looked at him and found herself quite drawn.

"Another time then?" Adam said and

walked with quite deliberate steps away from her.

Had Jenna been able to see his face she would have witnessed a determined rather than a defeated look.

Adam never one to walk away from a challenge determined that very afternoon he would have the seventeen year old Jenna on any terms. Adam was smitten. Completely and utterly smitten. Yes he thought. I will be sharing much more than a thick shake with you no matter how long it takes.

Chapter 3.

The courtship had been quick and the marriage orchestrated. Jenna's parents had set sail for their once in a lifetime world trip within hours of the honeymoon starting.

Adam had his girl until death do us do part. And Jenna? Well Jenna had found someone who represented stability, security, and made her feel valued. Love she realised later would be revealed over time. The deep growing old together kind of love. The being comfortable together kind of love. The having someone to go home to kind of love.

But the butterflies in the stomach kind of love that romance novels talked of? That feeling was to come many years later and it was anything but love, but even then it made an impact.

Jenna was sitting on her verandah reminiscing and asking herself if she had been too hasty in sending her visitor from the past away so quickly just weeks earlier. Looking across at the steers grazing in the paddock she scolded herself. "You were well rid of him then, don't go revisiting now."

With that thought Jenna closed her eyes took a deep breath and gave thanks for the life she and Adam had shared.

Whatever people said or thought, she and Adam had shared an amazing life and love had definitely been a part of it or so Jenna had thought, and even now Jenna was still believing, as each year passed their love had strengthened and grown. Jenna grew as a person and Adam? Adam seemed to have led a full life before he rolled into town, but new challenges and subsequent success defined Adam as more than a personable young man.

Adam and Jenna became an accepted couple in the circles of their small but developing community. Many people in the first months of their marriage waited for the baby to arrive, but there was no baby at that stage.

In fact it was a few years before babies arrived and although they arrived in rather quick succession there was absolutely no doubt as to their parentage.

Two were the spitting image of Adam in their youth and the third was a good mix of them both. Two boys and a girl. Adam had so wanted a girl. His sister had been killed when he was eight. He had told Jenna often as they lay together that he had always had fun with his older sister.

"Girls are so caring. You can talk to them. Boys are different. Completely different."

After his sister's death Adam had become the only child. So devastated by the loss of their daughter his parents had not had any more children.

Had Jenna given birth to a boy and a girl their family may very well have been complete at two. That was never discussed though. Like other details never discussed. How many children are we having? What type of house will we buy? Will we only own the one house? Will I go to work when the kids are at school? Will I continue to study when we are married?

Lots of questions that perhaps should have been asked, but the intensity and speed with which the courtship unfolded were never asked. Jenna was to be a wife. Adam her husband would provide for her. End of story. But like all stories the ending is unknown and the pages in between often contain surprises, unforeseen things, new people and events which shape the story, taking the reader along for the journey.

Jenna didn't know it but her role was one of a reader. Adam was the writer but the words he would write wouldn't always be seen or known. Adam was writing in invisible ink some of the time and Jenna was left out of many events.

Adam had in effect been writing multiple books, affecting multiple people, but what do they say? 'The truth always comes out in the end.'

Had Jenna known the ending she may very well have stayed in the library, immersed in her books.

Chapter 4.

June 26

It was now several weeks since the man of the bygone era had knocked on Jenna's front door and been sent away. Jenna had given little thought to him in that time keeping herself busy with the businesses she owned. She owned three in all and had been a hands on owner for many years.

When she engaged in her first business venture of writing cookbooks and giving cooking demonstrations the reaction from her children and friends was one of incredulousness.

"Jenna", her friend and neighbour Stella said sternly "you don't know the first thing about writing a recipe book let alone giving cooking demonstrations. Remember when you had to read out the passage at church just a few weeks ago? You were a wreck."

"Yes well I am not going to let that deter me. I have been taking photos of my food for ages. You know people need to see that food can be great and economical. Alison Holst is doing it very well."

"Pardon me but you are not Alison Holst."

Jenna approached a publisher and had two books published. 'Home Baking on a Budget' and 'Family Fare'. Both books did moderately well but the publisher asked Jenna to try her hand at writing a story about a family and let her have a look at it. "About 40,000 words should do it. Don't look at me like that Jenna you have flair. I wouldn't ask you to give it a go otherwise. Come on humour me?"

"All right Judy."

And so the novelist was born, well released and realised actually. Jenna started writing about what she did know, the antics of neighbours, children and friends and the more she observed and imagined the better her writing became and her books began to sell. Jenna was able to write during the day while her children were at school and was enjoying it immensely.

What helped Jenna was the readily available and accessible material. The new people who arrived in the neighbourhood and the change in the neighbourhood dynamic as a result. This always made for fresh ideas and lots of new adventures in her imaginative world.

Over the years Jenna had many books published and her 'hobby' became her work.

The children would go off to school, Jenna would do the dishes, hang out the washing, do vacuuming or dusting and at 10.00 a.m. she would sit down and write. Lunch was at noon and from 12.30 p.m. to 3.00 p.m. she would be writing four days a week. Even when the children were sick the routine didn't alter all that much.

As the children got older the routine gave Jenna the escape she needed from taking the children here, there, and everywhere and enabled her to add the changing people and stages in their lives to her writing.

Jenna didn't write masterpieces you understand, but her stories were entertaining and at times colourful and people read them for light relief. This pleased Jenna because she had enjoyed many hours of light relief writing them.

So Jenna pondered as she sipped her cup of Peppermint tea, how did her life end up being in such a pickle, by association as much as anything else? How indeed?

Chapter 5.

Chance is a fine thing. Sometimes chance is just that. It is when something happens quite by chance and goes well, leaving that happy fuzzy feeling with you for ages. Then there is a situation which can appear to have occurred by chance, but you get that feeling in the pit of your stomach which is telling you otherwise.

A contrived opportunity is not chance and Jenna had experienced that very thing that very morning.

Jenna had gone into town to pay her bills. When she was walking back to her car a man sitting at one of the outside coffee tables on the street stood up and said "What a surprise. We meet again. I will get you a coffee."

Jenna said "No thank you I am busy."

Looking directly at her with a smile on his face but with unsmiling eyes he said "We both know that you are not that busy. I thought if we spoke in a public place you may feel more comfortable?"

Jenna felt trapped. There was no surprise element in this encounter at all. He knew that on a Tuesday Jenna did not write. Tuesday was her to do day. To do the shopping. To pay the bills. To have a writing free day. It had always been Tuesday and Jenna had always gone into town on a Tuesday early as the shops and banks were opening. All that had changed over the years was that the supermarkets were opening earlier and ATM machines meant you seldom had to go into a bank at all.

"So how long have you been sitting there waiting?" Jenna asked.

"Let's just say I have enjoyed a leisurely breakfast."

"I see. In that case let's just say I don't want to have either a cup of coffee or a conversation with you." Jenna said with a force that surprised even her.

"We don't have to have either but I want to talk to you. There are things I need to say to you."

"Not today." Jenna said looking directly at him and seeing the look of determination returned to her own steely gaze. Jenna undeterred by this walked on.

Arriving in the car park Jenna began to feel a little unsteady on her feet and was thankful that her car was just two rows straight ahead and four parks along to the left. Once Jenna had arrived at her car and unlocked it, she put her shopping items on the back seat and had a good look around to make sure she had not been followed there. Taking a deep breath with her hand resting on the top of the car she satisfied that she had not been followed and she was now beginning to feel steady on her feet once again. Jenna climbed into the car and placed the key into the ignition. With a slight turn to the right the car started and Jenna put it into gear. Having a good look to each side of her, then checking her rear vision mirror Jenna slowly reversed out of her parking space and began the drive home. As soon as a thought about 'the man' popped into her head she consciously thought of something else, and given that the road was particularly busy that morning helped in that regard a lot.

Jenna arrived home. Put the car away. Walked into her house and sat on the nearest seat.   Quite some time passed before Jenna felt like moving and when she did her first priority was to put the jug on for a cup of tea.

KAREN PIVOTT

Chapter 6:

July 4th

It is of course American Independence Day and the usual stories were on the television about it. Even New Zealand on the other side of the world was included in this celebration, there was a shot of Kiwis in New York having a barbeque with their American neighbours to mark this auspicious occasion as Jenna was getting dressed.

As it happened Jenna was going to have the fourth of July this year to have something else to remember by. Jenna was giving a speech to the local council about the speed limit as the open road became the town road. For several years there had been debate about it. Last year there had been polarized discussion when a mother and her two children had been crossing the road in the 50km area and were hit and killed by a car going in excess of 80km per hour.

The driver was of course reducing speed from the 100 km zone just 80 metres prior to the accident having occurred. The law states you have 100m to slow down. It is debatable whether a further 30km per hour could have been reduced within the remaining 20 metres but that was irrelevant as far as Jenna was concerned.

Looking into the mirror Jenna said quite forcefully "You have a voice. You have been writing about this in the paper, and writing to officials for months, all you need to do now is speak to a small group of people who are able to do something tangible about the situation. I can speak about this without breaking down. I can be persuasive."

The face looking back didn't look in the least bit convinced.

Undeterred Jenna walked with determined steps to her car and drove into town.

There were many people gathered in the Council Chambers and the Councilors hearing the public submissions looked quite worn out before proceedings had begun.

The Chair of the Committee welcomed everyone and then people were able to contribute to the proceedings.

The whole affair was quite orderly and many people were heard including Jenna.

As on previous occasions Jenna had indeed found her voice 'under pressure' and her contribution was noted and commented upon along with many others.

All those involved in the process would find out what decision had been arrived at on the 18th of August.

Jenna called in to David's on the way home for a coffee with Deanna, but found David home instead.

"What a lovely surprise to find you home" Jenna said hoping her concern at finding him home was masked well.

"Yes and I will be home for a bit. Redundancies at work included me. I found out on Friday and it turned out Friday was the last day for all of us. I am still processing it all. The company hasn't handled it well. By not saying anything I wasn't looking for work and there is not a lot out there. Deanna is at a job interview now. Don't let me ramble on Mum say something. Just not why didn't you tell me?"

The tears that were welling up in David's eyes that then began to spill over and run uncontrollably down his cheeks, was more of a shock to Jenna than the news itself.

David was the steady one, the career driven, hard-working provider for his family.

"Why don't you make us a coffee and we will talk about what other options you could now pursue." Jenna said. A raised voice countered, "Did you not hear what I just said?"

"There is nothing wrong with my hearing David. You said you have been made redundant and Deanna is at an interview."

"I'll put the kettle on." David said as he made his way to the kitchen.

Jenna followed him all the while thinking of what options a construction engineer with a very large mortgage and a family to support could do in a depressed economy, where builders and property developers on the residential and commercial fronts, were going into receivership and liquidation on a daily basis.

They spent ages together. The silences being longer than the conversations and the kettle on the gas hob being filled and heated more than once.

The back door opened and Deanna walked in "I think it went well." She said. The relieved looks on both their faces prompted Deanna to say. "I know it's been awhile since I had a paid job but I'm not useless and I do remember how to answer and ask questions."

"Of course you do Deanna" Jenna said "It's just that I thought if we put the kettle on again I would never make it from here to my place without a couple of pit stops so my bladder thanks you for your timely arrival."

"Mum for goodness sake." David said and with Deanna laughing first and the others joining in Jenna knew that whatever the future held they would all get through it together.

Chapter 7.

On a sunny afternoon during a routine task, Jenna heard the phone ringing as she came along the path from her clothesline with a basket full of dry clothes. Reaching the back door she managed to open the door while balancing the basket, and get to the phone all be it a little puffed. Picking up the receiver saying "Hello." Jenna was greeted by "Hi Jenna. I got the job." Deanna said with excitement in her voice.

"I am so pleased. How's David?"

"David is fine. He has been offered a short term contract today so we are both celebrating. Would you like to come over? Say seven?"

"Try keeping me away." Jenna said with a laugh.

What a difference two weeks can make Jenna thought as she put the phone down.

Two weeks, yes two weeks she thought with a frown creasing her brow. What now seemed like a life time ago, within two weeks Jenna's world had been literally turned upside-down. The re-emergence of the boarder had unsettled her. David's redundancy. The final wash up of Adam's affairs and the inevitable moving forward phase looming all too quickly now. Still grieving and operating in a world of descending fog with lots to process and deal with.

What should have been a happy occasion was now another issue with Jenna was feeling quite swamped.

The purchase of Adam and Jenna's dream home was on the brink of being finished. A large sprawling Villa with even larger grounds, a swimming pool, tennis court and spa pool, new kitchen, several lounge areas and many bedrooms. Plenty of room for the family when they visit Adam had said as they strolled through it.

Jenna had fallen in love with it. It felt so right.

An offer was put in and accepted and then Adam had passed away suddenly.

That however was just the beginning. Adam's death brought with it many other shocks.

Funerals can bring out the best and worst in people. Funerals by their very nature are emotive occasions. Adam's was no different. All the family were in attendance.

Jenna had seen a woman and two small children dressed in black as they left the church where the service had been held. Unusually they were still at the cemetery long after most people had left.

Jenna went over to the woman introduced herself and asked how she had known Adam. Her reply sent Jenna into a state of utter shock followed by bewilderment. Jenna was seen taking a step back and appearing to lose her balance, her son David on seeing this ran over to steady her. Trying to regain her composure Jenna made an introduction.

"David this is Julia and her two children. Emma and Joshua. Your father's second family."

David went visibly white.

"Someone could have phoned me. If I hadn't read the paper I would never have known or was that the plan?" Julia asked in an accusatory manner. Jenna and David still trying to take the second family in looked blank. "You do know about us. You must. He told me all about the house he had bought you and that he had worked everything out." Observing glances of utter disbelief between Jenna, David and Julia then said "He didn't mention us? You didn't know anything about us?" Julia asked.

"No" Jenna said. Looking at this woman and her two children it was quite obvious to Jenna that this woman not only thought she had a right to attend the funeral, but felt she and her children should have been welcomed and accepted into the family fold.

"I don't mean to be cold but this is not the time. We well we all need time to come to terms with what has happened and clearly what we thought was going to happen."

"So we are supposed to just leave and disappear are we?" Julia said tears running down her cheeks and her voice rising.

"My mother has just buried her husband." David stated quite sternly "Perhaps this could be addressed another time?"

"I thought we had been addressed some time ago. I have waited and kept quiet, our children have a lost a father not just you." Julia said to David. "I was supposed to be marrying your father in a few months and you are dismissing me."

Jenna interjected by saying, "We are going back to the house. David perhaps you could move our group along so that Julia and her children can say their goodbyes privately."

"Yes, yes of course", said David realising he and Jenna weren't the only ones learning new information. David did move the group on and Jenna walked with Julia to the grave side leaving her and the children there and questioning whether she had ever truly known her husband at all. Today however wasn't a day for anger. Jenna had her children to comfort and care for. Adults they may be, but they too had lost a father, and David's children a grandfather, and Jenna felt that she had lost much more than a husband how much more would be revealed in time.

Chapter 8.

The reading of the will was the next surprise.

Both families were provided for, but the reality was that the second family had a freehold home in Julia's name.

Jenna's home was mortgaged to its maximum. The state of the bank accounts were the next revelation. Adam and Jenna's joint bank account was low. Julia feared much better with the money set aside for her in a bank account in her name only.

Jenna was reeling. The dream house had to be paid for in just four weeks.

The conversation became one of legal speak and in a state of shock Jenna realised that people had left the room and she found herself alone with Mr. Benton the solicitor.

"You have grounds to contest this Jenna, but it will be a long and expensive pursuit and there are no guarantees.

Adam's name is not on anything that Julia has".

"I don't know how I missed this. How could I not have known?" Jenna said speaking through a very thick fog.

"In my experience, and it is considerable I'm afraid to say, people who want to lead a double life do so extremely well. Deceit and deception become the norm. You have enough of your own money to buy your dream house", he said softly with his kind eyes looking directly at her.

"It was supposed to be our dream house." Jenna said quietly with a tear sliding slowly down her left cheek.

"I was putting quite a lot of my writing money into it, but the amount in the joint account now is laughable. Not in a funny way of course. I'm rambling. I can't believe this. There was the house money in there just a couple of weeks ago. I transferred the first part of the writing money over."

"When was this?"

"The day Adam went to the doctor for his annual check.   It was Adam who said 'look I am away for a few days shall we transfer some of that money over now for the house?' and I agreed. Do you think he knew he was going to die?"

"Now Jenna let's not get ahead of ourselves."

"What is left is only half of what I put in and the money that was already there is gone as well. He put it over to Julia didn't he?"

"It doesn't look like that. Jenna is there anything else that might help us unravel this puzzle."

"Puzzle is not a word I would use for this. I feel quite sick."

"Just sit there a moment and I will arrange for a cup of tea." Mr. Benton walked to the door and made his way to reception returning to Jenna quite quickly.

The tea dutifully arrived and with a very large spoon of sugar added to the cup in spite of Jenna's protest was drunk and the situation seemed to become a little clearer.

Mr. Benton looked gravely at Jenna and advised her to "go home and sit tight. I will be in touch. Money doesn't vanish there will be a paper trail somewhere."

Later in the day while sitting at home on her own the reality of the situation was still eluding her. It all seemed surreal. A woman she didn't know had two children to her husband. A house and money from her husband, which of course was all in her name.

By comparison Jenna had debt, and the debt exceeded the funds in the joint bank account and had reduced the equity in the property.

Then of course there was the dream house. The house Jenna had loved as soon as she had seen the leadlight door with the tulips on it that had been opened and had welcomed them into the interior of the large hallway.

Jenna was not about to give up on her dream and made the decision to go ahead with the purchase.

She would free some more money up from her "hobby account' and purchase the homestead for herself. The hobby account being both her hobby money and the inheritance from her parents and grandfather.

It was her grandfather who had opened the account for her originally and told her in a very serious tone, "Now young Jenna everyone has to pay their way. One day you will be working and probably married and you need to always have something put aside for yourself. Some money of your own. Life doesn't always end up the way we think it will."

Jenna could see her grandfather and what made her remember this wasn't the words. At eight years old those words have no meaning because at eight years old you don't have a relevant context to put them in do you?

No. It was the way he had said them and the misting over of his eyes as he looked down at her in a loving way that made her remember them all this time.

Back to the present and having made the decision to continue with the purchase, Jenna felt strangely free. This feeling of freedom had been aided by the Customer Services Manager Amanda at the bank who Jenna had gone to see. It appeared there was a short fall and a small loan would be needed to secure the purchase of the property. Amanda looked at all the relevant detail and determined that a loan would probably not be agreed to on the income Jenna was currently receiving. Jenna was visibly crestfallen.

"That shouldn't be a problem in the overall scheme of things" she said quite brightly.

"Let me get this right. I have to finalize the purchase of an expensive home. I have a shortfall and I cannot secure a small loan or mortgage from you based on my current earnings but that shouldn't be a problem?"

"Well Mrs."

"Jenna. Just call me Jenna."

"Well Jenna as I was about to say there is the Term Deposit that is up for renewal. The letter was sent out this morning."

"Oh. Um. That was for five years."

"And on Friday next week that five years is up. Let me see? Yes we could transfer the shortfall over to your savings account and perhaps reinvest the balance for you?"

"Do I have to reinvest it?"

"No. Perhaps once your financial situation is cleared up you could reinvest what is left over?"

Over the coming weeks Jenna worked through the financial mess Adam had left her, with during which time she had found Amanda at the bank to be extremely helpful. All the debt had been paid, the dream home purchased and some money reinvested.

Jenna had forgotten all about that money being put aside. Adam had done that. He had repaid Jenna the inheritance money that arrived unexpectedly from her Aunt Imelda in London. A short term business opportunity had been offered to Adam and money was tight at the time. It became clear to Jenna that Adam had not forgotten about it and knew it would be there. He no doubt had also taken into account the amount it would have grown in the last five years. Jenna felt herself getting used all over again, and had to fight off tears of frustration and anger rising rather quickly to the surface to join the ongoing feelings of hurt and betrayal. If I was writing a book she thought they would all be having a grand old party with a very large waterfall as the centre piece. Get a grip she admonished herself. You have things to do she remembered.

It did seem like a lifetime ago but it wasn't. It was a very real and painful part of her life which came several years after what had also been a rather dark patch and the reappearance of the person responsible for that was colouring the present.

"Don't dwell." Jenna told herself sternly. "You are about to celebrate with David and Deanna".

That said out loud Jenna busied herself with a light dinner then got dressed and left the house with an air of optimism.

Expect the good and good will come. A mantra which had been used by Jenna since the revelations about Adam had become known. His second family was only one of them.

Adam was gone now and Jenna had decided to move forward and not look back. Which even on a good day in all honesty was easier said than done.

Chapter 9.

The shift had been uneventful. Rather an anti-climax given the weeks leading up to it and Jenna found she was enjoying her home. Yes she reminded herself it was her home. Her dream home purchased with her money. The sale of their former home had been pretty much subsumed with the debt. Looking over her property, she appreciated the fact that her grounds were well cared for, and as maintenance free as possible. Since she had shifted in Jenna had made the gardens a priority for two reasons, winter was on the way, and gardening for Jenna was a tonic to be sipped daily. After the turbulence of the preceding months a tonic much needed.

Two months later it was August and

winter was well and truly underway. There had been much rainfall and walking through the grounds had been quite a squishy, squelchy experience.

The phone began ringing and Jenna walked through to the kitchen to answer it.

"Hi Mum it's Karla. I will make this brief. Bryce and I are coming home for Christmas if that is all right with you?"

"Of course. Oh how wonderful. You will be staying with me? It will be good to have someone else here for a bit, it seems like I have been rattling around here quite long enough already. When will you be arriving?"

"December 23rd if we can get the flights sorted. Love you and thanks. Can't wait to see you, it will seem like forever."

And with that the phone line went dead.

Jenna rang Deanna forgetting she and David were at work. The answer phone took her message. "Karla and Bryce home for Christmas. Christmas lunch at my place this year. Mum."

Taking a piece of paper from the drawer Jenna began making a list of what she needed to do for their arrival, writing furiously she stopped, looked at the list and wrote in capital letters "ENJOY THEM" and she knew she would.

If only Vincent and his wife Brittany would come for Christmas as well Jenna thought.

Vincent had gone to Canada to study and had then returned home for a couple of years. Then he got the phone call of a lifetime from one of the company's he had done some work experience with when he was in Canada, offering him a job.

Vincent who was flatting at the time spoke to his parents about it. They both encouraged him to make the move which he had done and he had never looked back.

Vincent had an extremely successful career as a commercial property architect and he did sculpture for relaxation. His relaxation became a successful second revenue stream for him and in this role he had met Brittany. Brittany did large metal pieces which were often incorporated into large commercial projects to bring balance to industrial areas or urban streetscapes.

After a whirlwind romance Vincent and Brittany married.

This was a good memory for Jenna. The trip over for the wedding was a truly happy occasion. The only overseas trip Adam and Jenna had done. A completely new experience that they had shared together.

Vincent and Brittany kept in touch via Skype and presents were exchanged on birthday's and at Christmas, but Jenna hadn't heard much from them since the funeral and they had left upset and feeling betrayed, and since then the ease of past conversations had been lacking, and the time between phone calls lengthening.

Jenna felt that Vincent blamed her for not knowing what Adam had been doing.

Jenna was reeling from revelations that seemed to be arriving on rolling waves from an unchartered sea.

Vincent didn't know the half of it, and if Jenna had her way he never would.

On impulse Jenna rang them to leave a message but to her surprise Vincent answered the phone.

"Hello."

"Vincent its Mum. Karla and Bryce are coming home for Christmas do you think you and Brittany could come to? It would be lovely to have a family Christmas altogether."

"Brittany's parents asked when we were going to see you. Look I need to say something. I felt, no I know that after the funeral I didn't handle that Julia stuff

well. Not well at all I'm afraid. I'm sorry
Mum."

"Who did?" Jenna began but was
interrupted by the words.

"Just hold on a minute would you I
think Brittany's home. Brittany?"

"Hi Vince I thought I would surprise
you and brought you lunch." Brittany was
saying in the back ground. "Mum's on the
phone she wants to know if we would like
to go over for a family Christmas, and
Karla and Bryce are going to be there. I
will put you on the speaker phone Mum"

"The whole family together at last in
the dream house sounds great to me."
Brittany said. "Could my parents come as
well? They want to see New Zealand."

"The more the merrier and I have
plenty of room." Jenna said.

"Okay I will talk to them and we will
get back to you on that, by the way how
did you know to ring today?"

"Well Bryce rang and I just thought
how great it would be if we were all
together this Christmas so I rang on an
impulse, and I was going to leave a
message but Vincent answered."

"Did he tell you why he's home?"
"No."

"Vincent has the measles. He's very
red and covered with a rash." Brittany

said.

"Have you seen a doctor?" Jenna asked.

"Yes", said Vincent "and although it is unusual for adults to get the measles it is not unknown. I am through the worst just resting up now. I will soon be back at work."

"What a joke that is" said Brittany "He hasn't stopped working he just hasn't been into the office. A holiday at Christmas is just what the doctor ordered."

"I am pleased I rang it's great to be able to speak to you both. Let me know about your parents Brittany it will be great to catch up with them. Love you both."

Jenna had literally just put the phone down when it rang. "What did you forget to tell me?" she said.

"I haven't had a chance to tell you anything yet." Mr. Benton said "I take it you were expecting a call from someone else. Shall I phone you back at a more convenient time?"

"No. I had just been talking to Vincent I thought he was phoning back. Mr. Benton what can I do for you?"

"Not a thing it is what I can do for you. Jenna I have located the missing funds. Adam had put them into a high risk investment to make a quick return and it appears he has done just that."

"Is that legal?" Jenna asked.

"Yes. Risky but very legal. You will be receiving an email from me with the amount you may expect once everything has gone through Probate. Oh and Jenna there were two amounts tied up. The other amount is due to mature in another twelve weeks. That return is looking quite sizeable as well. You will find overall that you have the original house equity and some back. And oh yes one more thing. Adam had two life insurance policies. You are the beneficiary of one of those as well."

"I didn't know that."

"I told you where money is concerned there is always a paper trail. I have to be honest Jenna I thought he had gambled funds away. He certainly had taken a gamble but not in the way I was fearing. Normally I would tell you this in the office, but I am about to head away overseas. I will get Carol to set up an appointment for you next month on my return."

"Thank you and enjoy your trip."

"I will and you may be able to plan a few of your own. You have family abroad as well don't you?"

"Yes. Quite unexpectedly it seems they are all coming home for Christmas this year."

As Jenna put the phone down again
she felt ten years younger, the hall mirror
told a completely different story, so she
took comfort in the fact that, as she
walked her steps felt lighter, and looking
through the windows the blue sky looked
very much brighter.

Chapter 10.

Jenna had been smiling on and off for days. Still grieving and with many days seeming to be interminably long, having a positive event to focus on was helping Jenna navigated her way slowly forward, and the revelation that the money was still there and had not gone completely as she had originally thought had helped in the overall scheme of things. Losing someone you have loved is never easy, and the grief process is just that a process that people work through, work with, or learn to live with. Jenna was determined to work through it.

Attending the odd weekend lunch with her family was part of that process, and Jenna was pleased she was making the effort to be there. Had she stayed at home she would have missed the opportunity, to see David, Deanna, Richard and Stephanie so excited. Stephanie now thirteen couldn't wait to spend time with her Aunty Brit. Stephanie had a very soft spot for Aunty Brit.

"You just don't get it dad." Stephanie had said over lunch one Saturday "Aunty Brit is so out there."

"Over there." David said with a twinkle in his eye.

"Seriously you are impossible." Stephanie said putting the salad bowl down a little more zealously than was necessary.

Richard being twelve just smirked which didn't help at all.

August became September and confirmation of the people coming and the arrival times had been confirmed and exchanged, and recorded on a list on the fridge so Jenna had ready access to them.

Stephanie phoned and suggested that she and Richard come over the following Saturday for the afternoon making individual Christmas Crackers for the family to enjoy on Christmas Day.

Jenna agreed and invited them for lunch. Jenna had done the menu for lunch knowing Richard would be pleased to spend time in the kitchen. Stephanie did the list of what the crackers would need and emailed that to Jenna. Over the coming week Jenna got what was needed.

Saturday arrived and Deanna dropped the kids off.

To spend a whole day with her grandchildren had always been a treat but today was especially good.

Stephanie organised the cracker making, Richard cooked lunch, and Jenna? Well Jenna enjoyed the blessing of the day and was grateful for it. Grandchildren are so special she thought and she had a sense of joy that for a very long time had eluded her.

"Nan." Richard said. "This is the first time this house will be full of people since you've lived here. Over Christmas I mean. It's going to be very noisy for you."

"Noisy? Yes I suppose it will." Jenna said.

The day seemed to speed by and in spite of herself Jenna felt a definite shift in her spirit. The fog was lifting. To have a celebration over Christmas in her new home would be a lot better than the more recent gathering the family had attended. Funerals are not joyous Jenna thought no matter what name you give them. "We are here to celebrate the life of Adam" Jenna recalled those words and asked herself quietly "Which life?"

"Nan." Richard called from the kitchen.

"I'm coming. What on earth are you two up to now?"

"We thought we could do spiced nuts for Christmas but we can't find the recipe. Which book are they in?" Richard asked.

"Well now." answered Jenna "That is a very good question. I honestly can't remember."

"Why don't we take a couple of books each and have a hunt through." said Stephanie.

"A hunt through don't you mean a look." Richard asked her.

"No I mean a hunt. On a hunt you will look properly. If you look you will do the boy's look and that will be a complete waste of time. Mum spoke to you about those shorts just this morning."

"Why don't the two of you see what you can find, I will go through my Christmas book and see if the recipe is in there. I will be back in a moment." Jenna said as she went in the direction of the spare room. On returning to the kitchen Jenna asked "Are the spiced nuts on the menu by any chance?"

"The menu. Oh we hadn't thought too much about doing up a menu for Christmas Day." Stephanie said.

"Christmas Day is the least of it. People will be here for Christmas Eve,

Christmas Day, Boxing Day, New Year's Eve, New Year and most of the days in between."

"We will be doing a lot of nuts then", said Richard with a very cheeky look.

"And dishes. I didn't think of that", said Stephanie. "Shall we do a roster up for the dishes?"

"I think you spend far too much time drawing up rosters." Jenna said and the three of them burst out laughing.

Jenna was genuinely sad to see them leave late in the afternoon. Today had been a very good day on all fronts and Richard certainly had a flair for cooking there was no doubt about that. He had prepared Jenna's evening meal while he was making lunch, and put it on a plate for her which he had covered and placed in the fridge. Jenna had discovered it there when she went to take the milk out to add to the coffee she had just made herself.

Sitting on her verandah soaking up the late afternoon sun, drinking her coffee and enjoying the grounds Jenna had the idea that she should make contact with Julia after the will had gone through probate. Jenna had questions she needed answered and Julia? On the two occasions Jenna had seen her, Julia looked as betrayed, hurt and confused as Jenna, and Julia had two young children to raise.

At least Adam had thought to take care of them financially Jenna found herself acknowledging which was easier to accept now as he had also made sure that Jenna was taken care of financially as well. Had Adam not died so suddenly Jenna would not have been any the wiser, and may have found herself facing a divorce instead of a death, in which case she would have suffered even more financial loss potentially if Julia's claim that Adam intended to marry her was correct, but that didn't make sense either because Adam had not filed for legal separation. Julia was being led along the garden path as well, and how long had she been on that path with Adam?

Oh Adam. Jenna thought you really were a piece of work.

Chapter 11.

September had passed by in a whirl literally.

Once the crackers were made the spring cleaning began. Cupboards were emptied out and cleaned. All unnecessary items were taken to the local church opportunity shop and by the middle of October Jenna was feeling extremely pleased with herself. This was to have happened prior to the shift of course, but things had been somewhat overlooked, or not dealt with due to the untimely death of Adam.

The house was looking good and she had managed to give a young man some much needed cash for his help in the spring clean.

Jenna had read about Jason in the local paper. He was a young man who had achieved well at school and was fundraising to go to an American College to study. Jason had been well on track with his parents help when his father had become terminally ill and died within a very short time. This had put financial pressure on the family.

Undeterred Jason had continued to fundraise with his goal entrenched in his mind and absolute faith that the means would be found in time.

One of his supporters set up an interview with the paper and Jason became very busy. No matter how much he worked the money coming in was insufficient due to his change in circumstance, and Jenna saw that as an opportunity.

Jenna had often seen opportunities in this way and helped people to improve their lot by becoming a partner with them.

Jenna had saved three small businesses in the town by this method adding a little extra to get a struggling business over the bump and becoming a silent investor unless called upon to give input of course. On paper this meant Jenna was now a multiple business owner. Which on paper looked correct but in reality wasn't really. The people who owned the businesses in the first place were still the people running the businesses so Jenna never saw herself as being an owner and the arrangement was always to pay the money back which with one business had just occurred and with business number two the repayments were nearing completion as well. Business number three, things were a bit up in the air there at present but nothing untoward was happening so Jenna was staying out of things there for the moment.

Helping a committed and focused student however was a new one for Jenna but Jenna felt this young man was in need of a helping hand.

Jenna had contacted the paper and met with Jason. Jason had become her fix it, clean it, get rid of it man and he was an extremely good investment. Always cheerful, often arriving early and doing extra time without expecting more pay.

Jenna was encouraged by Jason's attitude and spent a lot of time with him over the course of their days working together.

Jenna gave Jason a cheque for the balance he needed and he was speechless very possibly for the first time in his life.

"I have no idea how I can pay or work all this off" he said.

"Jason I believe in you. This is for you to do your studies and you can repay me by completing your studies and being a good citizen." Jenna said "Oh and the windows will be ready for another wash when you are home on holiday. I expect you to keep in touch I want to know how you are doing."

"I don't know when I will be back."

"That's ok, now off you go as your mother will have your dinner ready for you. See you Saturday?"

"What about tomorrow afternoon?"

"I think you have a College payment to make." Jenna said to Jason with a smile on her face, "See you Saturday."

Jenna watched Jason ride away on his bike and knew she was going to miss him when he went but that was months away yet. Instead of getting a very sad feeling, Jenna got a very good feeling welling up from the pit of her stomach.

"I am so thankful I can help people. Thank you, thank you. Thank you." Jenna said out loud and the large Copper Birch tree shook in agreement. Jenna had to thank Adam as well because knowledge of his life insurance policy enabled Jenna to give some financial assistance in the first place.

Jenna slept very well that night. Very

well indeed.

The following morning Jenna decided to phone Julia. The will had not yet gone through probate but Jenna felt the time was right. With a firm resolve she picked up the phone and dialed Julia's number.

"Hello." a young girl's voice answered.

"Yes hello. I would like to speak to Julia."

"Mum. Mum it's for you. A lady on the phone.", and with that a clank onto a hard surface possibly a table met Jenna. Muted footsteps could be heard and then "Yes hello. I'm sorry about that. I am trying to get her to bring the phone to me."

"Yes they are always in a rush at that age aren't they? It's Jenna, Julia. I was wondering if we could talk. Meet somewhere perhaps and talk?"

"Jenna. Oh I see. Is it about the money?"

"No I feel we have dealt with all that. No I wanted to ask you some questions about Adam."

"Do you know I have been trying to get the courage up to phone you and ask you the same thing. I am free next Wednesday perhaps we could meet for lunch I know a place about halfway between us."

"Wednesday will be fine say eleven

forty five before the rush?"

"Do you have a pen?" And with that Jenna wrote down the address and lunch was confirmed.

Jenna felt good about making contact and hoped that both of them could come to some place of acceptance and healing. Jenna knew however that it would take more than one lunch to do that.

Chapter 12.

October had arrived and Jenna had her Christmas shopping well in hand.

Jason was pruning, weeding and mowing the lawns amongst other things. His college fees were paid and Jenna noticed how much more relaxed he was in his approach to things. He was working well, with the strain around his eyes visibly gone now.

"Jason I think you should take a couple of weekends off so you can study. Look on it as paid leave for professional development."

"I don't think that's fair. I can still come."

"Who's the employer? Take the next two weeks off from here and study, spend time with your mum, go to a movie it's only two weeks."

"What about the lawns?"

"The lawns are they going somewhere?" Jenna asked with a smile.

Jason shook his head and smiled "Okay and thank you."

Jenna had received a call from Alan at the book shop the business number three she had an interest in.

"Jenna would it be possible for us to have a meeting?"

"Of course Alan when would suit you?"

"Could you manage later today?"

"How about when the shop closes at 5.00 pm?"

"Thank you Jenna see you then."

Jenna put the phone down and felt that things were about to change. She didn't know how but she would find out soon enough.

Jenna left to go to the shop in good time and when she arrived it was about ten minutes to five. Alan was not his usual relaxed and happy self so Jenna decided to leave the banter on this occasion. There were no customers in the shop so Jenna closed the door behind her and put the closed sign across the door.

"How can I help Alan?" Jenna said looking at his anxious face.

"Help is all you have done Jenna since our very first meeting."

"What do you need?"

"Time. My mother is failing Jenna and I need to be with her. I think it's time I sell the shop or at least my interest in it."

"Okay. Let's put it on the market."

"You don't want to buy me out? Robyn would make a good Manager."

"Let's put it on the market and see what happens. Do you want to take some leave? We could get Robyn to run things while you are away."

"Thanks but no. Once I go I won't be inclined to come back. New chapter you know all about that."

"Absolutely. If things change, we will change things around okay?"

"Thanks Jenna. I'll ring Peter he does commercial property sales."

"Let me know when the meeting is not a Tuesday."

"Your doing day. Yes I remember."

Jenna smiled and left the shop. In the car she thought about being the sole owner of the shop and having Robyn manage it for her but decided against it.

A new owner will be there for the shop Jenna thought and drove home with a very good feeling about it all.

This was not a bad thing, the money for the shop could be put to other uses and Jenna still had one business she had a financial interest in and a book to finish. Yes life was busy enough just now nothing was happening in small measured doses these days. The money was confirmation of that. From potential financial ruin just a few months ago to affluence, before the Will was through probate.

Jenna was on the brink of change. She had felt that for some time but could not put her finger on what that change was. Perhaps the sale of the book shop was it or maybe that was just a part of it?

Chapter 13.

Jenna had felt there was change coming at the beginning of October. The sale of the book shop business happened very quickly, in fact within ten days of it being listed. The feeling of impending change did not ease at all.

Labour Weekend arrived and Jenna, thanks to Jason's help during the week, had accomplished all the chores she had intended to do over the weekend so she decided to have some rest and recreation this took the form of a visit to the local video shop, resulting in renting some DVD's, then visiting the library and taking out a historical novel. No rest and recreation session would be complete without nibbles, a bottle of wine and friends.

As spur of the moment as it was,

Jenna had three longstanding friends who would be attending on the Saturday for a 'girls' day. Not one of them hesitated or refused the invitation when Jenna phoned them on that Thursday evening.

It had been years since they had all got together for recreational purposes only, and Jenna was quietly excited while actively engaged in getting ready for their arrival.

"Where would I be without friends?" She asked herself, already knowing the answer.

Jenna had always been supportive of people especially her friends, but when the dark clouds hovered with the Curtis situation, and here he was again popping into her present, and then her husband's double life being revealed, Jenna knew exactly who her real friends were and they were an invaluable asset to her in those times.

Jenna had herself over the years been a great asset to them in times of need and their loyalty to her was still appreciated.

Yes a rest and recreation day with the 'girls' was just what she needed. They were all over fifty five now but still 'girls at heart'. Jenna's Gran would say "It's only a number", when she headed off into town on the bus.

Jenna didn't have much time with her Gran when she was young. There were sayings she remembered which at the time had no relevance to her, but with life experiences they had become meaningful. Gran was right age is just a number.

Jenna thought of some young people who were older than she was. Older, because they walked around with the troubles of the world on their shoulders. Everything seemed to be a problem.

Jenna had always been a solution based person acknowledging a problem then looking beyond it to find solutions.

This infuriated people who wanted a sympathetic ear and validation. Jenna always provided a sympathetic ear but her mind was always at the next step, the solution step so the validation didn't always happen. Jenna did help people though, those people who wanted to be helped.

"We are all so different." Jenna said out loud.

Jason was a case in point. Jason could have given up on his dream but he carried on until he found a solution, and he found a solution because he expected to have one, Jenna just happened to be part of it, and what a joy it was having his help and his company. I am truly blessed Jenna thought and gave thanks for that.

Chapter 14

The Labour Day weekend passed all too quickly and it was soon November. A favourite time of year for Jenna the month before the holiday season really began.

Each year Jenna would make sure all her Christmas shopping was done by the end of November. All the cards for posting were filled in and envelopes addressed.

Presents were purchased and the cards to go with them written.

Jenna had a book and wrote a name beside every present she bought because if she saw something that she knew a particular person would enjoy Jenna would purchase it there and then which typically made the shopping spree in November redundant because Jenna had pretty much bought for everyone by then.

This year Jenna had just two people left to buy for. Two important people Jason and herself.

It was on the second Tuesday of November when Jenna walked past "Bits of This and That" a new shop. Jenna was curious so she went in. She browsed for a time then her eye caught an interesting picture on the wall.

An embroidered picture of Harvard. Jenna couldn't resist and promptly purchased it for Jason.

Only one present left to buy she thought and merrily set off on her way home with the picture securely under her arm.

Jenna had just finished unloading the car and was in the kitchen preparing to make herself a coffee when there was a knock on the front door.

Jenna walked through to answer it knowing that whoever was there would be a surprise because Jenna wasn't expecting anyone.

Jenna opened the door to a very well dressed slender man in his late thirties Jenna guessed. A salesman type. Just what I need Jenna thought.

"Good morning. You don't know me so I will introduce myself."

Jenna expecting a sales pitch raised her hand and said "Please let me save us both some time. I do not need to purchase anything and I have my own religious beliefs."

"Me too." He said with a smile. "I am not here to sell you anything, actually I am here to buy something."

"That's interesting" Jenna said "because I don't believe I am selling anything. If it is about the shop, that has been purchased already and I don't break agreements with people."

"No, no it's not that. Oh dear I am mucking this up. Well the truth is I didn't know I was buying either but then I came here. May I start over? "

"Let me help you. You had said Good morning. You don't know me so I will introduce myself." Jenna said to him with a smile.

"Yes. I am Mason Andrews my grandparents raised me here. My happiest days have been in this house and on these grounds and I was wondering if I could walk around the property."

"Yes of course. That is no problem at all. I have just made a coffee would you like one?"

"Yes I would thank you. What I was going to say originally was that I want to buy the place, selling it was a mistake. I acted rashly. A mistake I made in a time of sadness some years ago, that I hope can be fixed."

Jenna was gob smacked "I'll have an extra spoonful of coffee in my cup I think. I was not expecting this."

"Me either can you make mine the same please?"

And there it was the change completely out of the blue. The change that Jenna had felt was coming in early October.

Change was like love really a tangible thing with timing quite unexpected. It would be there then present itself somehow either in your face, or by sneaking up on you. This was definitely an unexpected and in your face experience, but strangely Jenna wasn't put out or surprised it felt completely right. When she had first seen the house with Adam they had plans that included having lots of people staying and visiting, but that had all changed and would never happen that way now.

Mason walked around the grounds. Jenna took him through the house which had changed and had been modernized since he had lived there.

The kitchen had been added and was new when Jenna purchased the property. There was a spa pool in its own room. A double garage and workshop replaced the single garage and carport that had been there originally.

And over coffee Mason gave a walk through account of what had been. The wallpaper in his bedroom had been blue with aero planes on it and changed for his fourteenth birthday.

Jenna realized this young man not only loved the house, but the two people who had given him a home very much indeed.

Sitting there listening to him recount his adventures and memories of the house while he was growing up Jenna realised that this house needed to be loved and here was a young man who loved it very much and had a need for it.

What the family would say about it never entered Jenna's head. She sat and listened some more and got swept along on the nostalgic story of Mason Andrews and what a very interesting story it was. Jenna could not have written a better tale herself and that was saying something.

CHAPTER 15

Jenna had been thinking about Mason's offer.

Mason had been away overseas working for many years and had come back when his grandparents had been poorly. He attended to their needs and after their deaths which were very close together he had returned overseas to work.

Mason had thought that was the answer. Work and more work and getting rid of the house and the pain of the loss was how he had coped with everything at the time.

Mason had done very well on his return to the trading floor and had made lots of money. He was trading in a boom time and he managed to do very wise things with his money and grow it at that time.

The years passed and Mason felt a pull to return to his homeland. He was at a bar one night having a quiet beer after a very busy day when a young woman plonked herself on the stool beside him.

"Lemon, lime and bitters please." She asked the bartender. Her long brunette hair spilling down her back, as she removed her hat.

"Don't you just love these winters in good old England?" She asked Mason.

"Yes I do." He replied

"Hi, I'm Amanda. What part of New Zealand do you come from then?" She asked picking up on his accent.

"Auckland then the Waikato and I'm Mason."

"I'm from Whakatane and I've had a day where I really miss home"

"Me too."

"Have you eaten?"

"Well no I didn't really feel like food."

"Me either but I will be ready after this drink. Why don't we have dinner together and reminisce about home?"

"Why not?"

They were married eight months later and they both decided it was time to return to New Zealand.

Mason had looked into doing consultancy work with his financial skills and be based at home and Amanda was happy to be a stay at home mum if they got pregnant.

And the pull to the happiest place he had ever lived began.

Jenna was embarrassed by the offer. It was much more than she had paid and even with the more recent valuation done she felt it was generous but Mason wanted the property and insisted. His reasoning was that had Jenna stayed longer she would have made a capital gain. After all Jenna was not thinking about shifting out, she had barely moved in.   Mason said the money he was prepared to pay made allowances or compensation for all of that.

Jenna decided that having shifted in and lived there on her own, with this Christmas being the first time she would have all the family there and probably the only time she would have them all together, for a very long time. What would Adam be making of all this? Old habits die hard they don't just die out with the person who has left you.   Sitting and thinking long and hard, weighing up her list of the positives and negatives about staying and going, Jenna came to the conclusion her dream life in her dream home was not what she had thought it would be. How could it be? It was supposed to be their dream life in their dream house. Her and Adam's plans, life, all that had died with Adam and the going on stoically in 'my dream home' was not Jenna's dream home at all, and that was the absolute, stark naked truth of it. Jenna rang Mason and said. "Would February be all right? I have the family staying with me for Christmas and I need to find a place."

"March would suit us better."

"March 12th?" Jenna asked.

"March 12th. I will send you the paperwork. Thank you Jenna." Mason said and hung up.

Well now I've done it Jenna thought. I have lost a husband. Bought and shifted into my dream home and sold it within a very short period of time quite out of character so why am I feeling this is the right thing to do? Change, change, change and yet even with the need to find a new place in which to live then shift Jenna felt there was still more change ahead.

I am like a rising waterway moving along the current of life swiftly and picking up debris wanted, unwanted, useful and discarded. Each corner represents change and sooner or later the sea will appear. I will be swept onto the vast sea and float. The change will stop and life will be manageable, calm, never boring again, but settled. With this analysis in the forefront of her mind she set about the mundane task of vacuuming to the William Tell Overture playing on her mp3 player through her headphones.

The next place will be smaller. Smaller house. Smaller grounds. Jason. Yes she thought as she hummed and started planning what she would be looking for in a home. She would need to have something for Jason to do when he came home.

The mental list of who to call and go out looking with. Where to look. What to look for. Well there was no rush it was months away yet just a general enquiry and nose about would do for now she thought and, with the music playing Jenna soon got through her vacuuming. What normally was spread over two days she had done in the afternoon and when she put the cleaner away and went to the fridge to get her things out for dinner the phone rang.

"Hi Mum thought we would pick you up and take you out for dinner."

"What's the occasion?"

"Because we can and we want to. Be there in half an hour."

KAREN PIVOTT

CHAPTER 16

Jenna scrolled through the real estate websites to have a look at houses and saw a couple that she thought may suit her well.

Modern. Brick. With landscaped easy care grounds. Four bedrooms. Internal garage. What a treat she thought not having to get out and slosh about in the rain when you arrive home. Being able to take the groceries from the car to the house without tripping up the stairs, or getting cold and wet.

Jenna glanced down to the reminder note in front of the computer which brought her back from the clouds and firmly in the realm of reality "deadline submission of novel 2nd December."

Jenna sat at her computer and clicked on her novel, and continued editing. By late that afternoon the manuscript was complete and sitting in a courier delivery bag.

Jenna picked it up and headed out the door.

Tonight would be good as she was taking her two grandchildren out for dinner. They had requested Mexican. This was a tradition when a book was sent off to the publisher Jenna would take them out for a bite to eat.

Over the years that bite had changed from a morning tea on a Saturday, to lunch before afternoon Kindergarten School, and now dinner. The amount of the bite had changed markedly to by way of cost and amount as well.

Easy to forget how much a teenager can eat when they are relaxed and not rushing here and there. Easy to forget what good company they can be when they're not rushing here and there. Easy to forget how thoughtful they can be at times as well.

They had asked Jenna if she would like to invite Jason to join them which had surprised her, but she had said no.

"It is our special time and I don't feel we need to share it." Jenna not only said that but believed it.

When she was raising her children they all had one on one special time through the month on one occasion every month. This was not always easy to manage but Jenna scheduled it in to her diary. Jenna felt it was important to have that time with her children on her own.

Mostly they did things together. What Jenna gained from that was good lines of communication with her children as they were growing up and she was proud of that.

The interruption to that time occurred when the boarder moved in. The dynamics changed completely.

Jenna paused and thought about the visitor she had turned away earlier in the year. The ex- boarder who had sought her out in the main street. The man who seemed to keep popping into her head. Maybe Jenna should have aired things with him. Maybe Jenna should accept she missed things because she herself was distracted. Adam being away more than usual. Just let things lie. Yes that would be the sensible thing. No sense in dredging it all up again even though bits of it didn't add up or make sense.

But even with that thought Jenna knew deep down it wasn't going to just go away. She felt a reprieve was all she had, and was not sure how long even that would last.

Jenna was intuitive and usually her intuition was right.

What Jenna didn't know then was that she was blocking the healing she needed.

Jenna also didn't have a crystal ball, but she knew it wasn't done with and oh how she wished she could close that door completely.

Jenna took stock of her thoughts and readied herself for her night out. The grandchildren were waiting for her and had both made an effort with their appearance as usual. Jenna was very happy about that. No matter when you saw them they were clean, neat and tidy with their pants or trousers sitting at their waist not down by their thighs.

They got into the car chatting away and chatted throughout the whole evening. Even the getting into the car had improved over the years Jenna thought as she drove them home. No fighting about who had the front seat. They took turns independently these days. No arguing, no fuss at all.   Yes she smiled to herself they are both growing up quite quickly now. Where do the years go?

After dropping them off, on the drive home Jenna took a detour, and drove just outside the town boundary parking in a rest area which looked over the township. Jenna sat there in the quiet and looked across at the town. The night lights have told their own story over the years Jenna thought. The town is definitely expanding. It used to be town meets country years ago when the lifestyle block boom had occurred. Now she thought its country meets town. The lifestyle blocks of five to ten acres were now part of the town as well.

CHAPTER 17

November had become December with no fan-fare at all. Just a natural gentle progression. One day it was November and the next day December had begun.

Jenna was sitting on her deck enjoying her breakfast coffee when the phone rang.

"Good morning Nan it's December. It is just so exciting isn't it? All the family together soon and I can't wait." Stephanie's excited voice tumbled down the telephone line.

The silence must have been deafening for Stephanie because what she said next surprised Jenna immensely

"You are pleased they're coming aren't you?"

"Yes of course. Of course. I just hadn't realised we had reached December.

Where has the year gone?"

"Nan we were talking about this the other day."

"I know but where have the days gone between then and now can you tell me that?"

Stephanie giggled "Nan can I bring my presents and wrap them at your place this weekend?"

"Of course you can but I don't think you need to be worried about not having any presents, there will be plenty to go around so why are you wasting your money on buying yourself presents?"

"You are having coffee aren't you Nan? I think I will buy you herbal tea for your present. No caffeine in herbal tea it is good for you."

"See you Saturday. Would ten o'clock suit you? I need to have a couple of coffees before you arrive so I can keep up."

"Nan, you do have Christmas paper there don't you. It's just that well."

"Yes Stephanie I have Christmas paper here and small cards."

"Thanks Nan."

And just like November sliding into December Stephanie was off to the next thing in her thirteen year old world.

Jenna knew all too well that in that world Stephanie would have spent every cent on presents and not considered the cost of paper, cello tape or cards when she was buying her presents. Jenna also knew that her father David would not have been happy about that, but then Jenna reflected on David and the world he was living in at thirteen.

He was such a very serious, very studious boy. All his energy went into school and sports. The fact that he had loyal friends always amazed Jenna because David was the least social of her three children.

Reflecting, reminiscing what good does that do Jenna chided herself.

Her eyes drifted to the window. She gazed with absolute appreciation on the scene before her. A lush carpet of grass and beyond that her small paddocks. Jenna marveled at the few sheep, and lambs that were munching away seemingly without a care in the world.

Idyllic she thought gratefully. This is an idyllic property no wonder Mason felt at peace here and wanted to return home.

Jenna had decided to donate two of the sheep to the food bank for needy families, and have one sheep for her own family while they stayed over Christmas.

A good old fashioned traditional family Christmas dinner.

Back to Stephanie and what she had asked, "You are pleased they're coming aren't you?"

"Yes" Jenna said out loud "I am very pleased they are coming," as she continued to drink her coffee and began writing a list of all the things to be done for their arrival.

Ring the home kill butcher and book him in was the first thing on her list. Make up all the beds. Air the rooms and the list got longer and longer. Thank goodness Jason was still coming on Saturdays and had offered to do a few days during the week around his exams. Yes maybe I will take him up on that offer of next Tuesday Jenna thought and added phone Jason about next Tuesday to her list. Tuesday was the to do day and what Jenna had to do was a very large shop to get stores in and Jason would be able to help her with that and a few other things.

Hearing the clock chime ten Jenna knew it was time to get moving and start her day in earnest. The jobs for today were on the magnetic pad on the fridge. I admonished Stephanie for rosters recently she thought, and here I am with lists for things to do, lists for daily jobs, and David has planners and lists all over his office. No wonder Stephanie is good at rosters the poor girl is rostered, and listed out and not yet fourteen.

Perhaps Jenna though later I will get Stephanie a wall planner to go with her Christmas present so she can have everything in one place, and chuckled away. Yes Stephanie would like that it would make her feel really grown up.

I wonder if Stephanie keeps a diary? Yes I will get her a diary as well why not, that will balance the money I have spent on them. Richard did better this year in monetary terms and Jenna was always conscious of keeping those matters as equal and as fair as possible. One child should never be more valued than another that had been and still was Jenna's philosophy. "If we spend twenty dollars on a birthday present for one that is what we spend on all the birthday presents for the children this year." Jenna remembered that conversation with Adam when David was coming up to his tenth birthday. Adam had seen a helicopter which was on special for twenty dollars reduced from forty five dollars. At the time the amount spent on birthday presents had been fixed at fifteen dollars. This was one of the few occasions Jenna had spoken up.

"Yes." she said "It is reduced but the others will see a forty five dollar helicopter.

If you are going to spend an extra five dollars on David we spend twenty dollars on each of them this year." It was also one of the few times Jenna had got her way.

As it happened that year all the children got presents reduced so they all did very well for their twenty dollar gifts that year, and Adam made sure he got good value for money for his twenty dollars.

Jenna didn't know how but children seemed to sense injustices like that, and those injustices tended to grow and could take on a life of their own. She had witnessed this first hand with the neighbours and vowed it was not something she would do. Life had a way of presenting enough issues for people over time so adding to them didn't seem necessary. Birthday and Christmas presents were two areas where joy, happiness and pleasure could be easily achieved so why would you want to create issues there?

CHAPTER 18

Jenna had all the Christmas paper and small cards in the dining room ready for Stephanie's arrival and right on the dot of ten o'clock Stephanie was dropped off by David who was in between jobs that morning.

A quick wave, the door closing and Stephanie was bounding up the steps with bags and boxes precariously balanced. So eager was she to wrap these items and get into the house to do so she nearly collided with Jenna on the porch.

"Oh hi Nan."

"Would you like some help with those?" Jenna asked.

"No thanks I've got it covered. Dining room?" Stephanie asked.

"Yes the table is ready for you. Careful Stephanie. How about I go ahead of you and make sure the doors are wide open?"

"Okay but I can push them open with my foot."

"And drop the boxes and topple over?"

"Nan!" Stephanie exclaimed.

"Yes you're right it is the doors I should be more concerned about after all no one warned them that whirlwind Steph was arriving today. There you are." Jenna said as she opened the door completely for Stephanie. "Does that help?"

"Thanks Nan."

Stephanie got straight into the sorting, wrapping and labeling of her presents for Christmas while Jenna began the fruit mince for the Christmas mince pies.

Jenna was quietly bemused by Stephanie's industrious effort. So engaged was she that she forgot all about food which for a teenager is really quite something.

Fortunately for Stephanie Jenna had lunch sorted and managed to get both the lunch laid on the porch table and Stephanie sitting at a chair in a timely manner.

"You seem to be making great

progress." Jenna said as Stephanie munched away on a freshly made salad sandwich.

"Yes I think so. It is taking longer than I thought it would. Do you have any bows or that curly stuff. They look a bit plain the ones I've wrapped."

Jenna's response was to say "It's the love that goes into the present that counts."

"Yes that's why I need to do more to make them look pretty so people know I've really put some thought into it."

"Another sandwich?" Jenna asked with a smile knowing that Stephanie had missed her point altogether. Still insight isn't always present on the day is it, she thought, especially not when you are focused on wrapping presents, and have been interrupted by lunch and conversation, which is all a bit much really in the scheme of things.

Jenna let her eyes wander from her grand-daughter and over to her roses. They were blooming very nicely and the wind was picking up their scent which was wafting in the direction of the porch and was quite delightful.

I wonder if my new place will have roses? Jenna thought. Finding a new place had proved somewhat more of a challenge than Jenna had anticipated and decided on the advice of the Real Estate Agent to leave until January "You have plenty of time there is no rush. The right place will come up. People are in holiday mode now."

Yes they were Jenna conceded but that wasn't helping her in the quest to find a new place.

To be fair though Jenna was herself concentrating on the family visit which was getting closer as the days passed by.

So it was quite a surprise that the house thing sorted itself out for her one could say.

CHAPTER 19

The weeks of December had literally flown by and Jenna found herself reading the calendar and looking at the date circled which reminded her when the additional family members were arriving for the Christmas celebrations from overseas, the 23rd of December.

Jenna realised that was just two days away and although the house was ready was she?

This was a legitimate question to be asking one's self after a lengthy period of distance from your offspring.

Yes they had been over for the funeral, but they had been disbursed between the wider family over that time. This time they would all be under the one roof and that would be quite different.

They leave you at one point in their life and under a set of circumstances at

that time and return in well quite another.
Jenna thought.

Time changes people. Circumstances
change. Experience is often added into
the mix and voila like watching a magic
show you literally don't know what is
going to come out of the mix.

The phone rang which deflected these
thoughts and Jenna answered it with her
usual "Good morning you are speaking
with Jenna"

"Well I shouldn't be" said Stephanie
"You are meant to be taking me to the
dentist and we might just make it if you
leave now."

Jenna put the phone down and
picking up her handbag and keys, went
straight to the garage to get into the car
and make her way to pick Stephanie up.

How on earth had she forgotten that
she thought as she was driving and then
another thought popped into her head, the
appointment with the lawyer on the house
Jenna was buying. Yes she was to attend
to that at the same time as Stephanie was
at the dentist.

Although initially miffed by
Stephanie's tone Jenna was now grateful
that Stephanie had phoned her.

Everyone arriving and all the
preparations Jenna you need to go back to

making lists, she admonished herself
mentally as she pulled up to a waiting
Stephanie.

"Sorry if I was rude on the phone. I
didn't mean to be rude I was just getting a
bit anxious. You are always early you
see."

"Yes I do see. I forgot Stephanie."
Jenna said rather more harshly than she
intended and pulled back into the traffic.

Stephanie made it to the dentist with
two minutes to spare Jenna calculated if
she ran up the stairs which she usually
did.

Jenna parked the car and made her
way to the office of her lawyer.

"Jenna come in. You are looking
well."

"You are not looking so bad yourself.
How are the family?"

"Fine, fine, and yours?"

"I will be able to answer that after the
23rd. They are arriving on mass. Now
let's get this paper work signed up shall
we?"

"I have it all here ready for you. What
do the family think of your move?"

"They don't know yet. In fact I don't
want them to know yet so if you could
accommodate me in that I will be very
pleased."

"Jenna?"

"Yes I know what you are going to say. They or at least one of them should know, but on this occasion it is not going to be the right thing as far as I am concerned. They will all be living overseas by my shifting in date and I think it best at this stage to keep this move to myself."

"But the family home?"

"And there-in lies the irony in its completeness. This will be the first and last time the whole family will be in this home, and my last remaining son, daughter in law and grandchildren are leaving for Australia shortly after Christmas so there it is. A very large home with one person rattling about in it for the vast majority of the time. A home needs to be lived in properly and now it will be. A win, win, all around."

"When did you find out about David shifting overseas?"

"Last night. The company are transferring him to their Sydney office. Not even their children know yet. They shift over late in January. They are telling their children tonight."

"About this house?' He asked looking at Jenna who was nodding "So long as you are sure."

"I am sure. I was not so sure about

my current home at the time of that purchase and it has worked out reasonably well until now. The grandchildren have had plenty of room to muck about but they are going and I need a change. The family home will be wherever I am, I guess if the family need to visit a family home, but as with you and Anne our family have their own families now."

"Yes. If you sign here and here."

Which Jenna did with an unusually lightened heart.

Mr. Benton meant well and had looked after her interests especially through the difficult times, but these days Jenna was content and was determined everyday upon waking that there would be no more difficult times of her making at all.

104

CHAPTER 20

The Christmas and New Year holiday period with its chaos had abated and all visiting family members had vacated and arrived safely home once more to embrace and engage with their lives.

David and Deanna were staying at Deanna's family home while her parents were away which worked out perfectly for them as their home had been packed up and emptied with their belongings crossing the Tasman sea for their new lives in Australia.

Just two days to go thought Jenna and the last of our family will be leaving our shores.

Stephanie and Richard had been biking around regularly and there was a family dinner planned for the last night which Jenna had the ingredients for, but all of a sudden Jenna just wanted to sit on her decked porch and purvey the grounds with a cup of tea.

Nestled comfortably in her chair on the porch she marveled at how similar the view now was to the view she would enjoy at her new property.

Green grass, stock grazing, old trees, border gardens and established grounds, she was truly blessed.

The houses were different of course. Jenna acknowledged and embraced that difference. A one hundred year old villa is not the same as a modern brick home on a concrete foundation, but both homes were roomy and had plenty of natural light due to their generously large windows.

Jenna had her thoughts interrupted by the sound of a vehicle. She wasn't expecting anyone so she rose and made her way to the front door where she could hear someone knocking.

Jenna opened the door and there he was once again standing in front of her.

"Before you tell me to leave I just want you to know I am very grateful to you and your family for including me in your lives. Not to mention what Karla did recently. I have spoken to her directly. I told her I would make one last attempt to see you, talk to you."

"She didn't say."

"I asked her not to. I.....I had to come and do this in person. I am sorry Jenna for all of it. I lost my way. No excuses."

"Would you like to come in? I have tea."

"You always have tea of various kinds with the occasional coffee on hand and Milo from memory, but no. No thank you. I am leaving this island. I have an opportunity to live in the Marlborough Sounds and I am taking it. I wanted to say I miss you and I wish you well. You deserve to be happy."

"Thank you. I am happy and about to shift myself into a smaller place and modern."

"Karla didn't mention that."

"The kids don't know yet. I will tell them when I'm settled."

There was a pause and as the visitor turned to leave Jenna said "Curtis I too could have handled things better. Not taken the high moral ground without all the facts. Karla spoke to me at length. You know before you came into our lives I had one to one time once a month with our children and they would tell me all sorts of things. When you shifted in that all stopped. Our lives changed and as a result our children formed new and different alliances. I was shocked by what Karla told me, what she had been holding onto for her friends and how conflicted she had been for many years, but I am proud of her. She revisited that time and spoke up which has helped you. I feel a complete failure as a mother. I not only wasn't there for her I didn't know she was in need of me. How's that for high moral ground?" Jenna spat at him with feelings of guilt swamping her.

"Jenna you were right to take the moral high ground. No one else bothered. It became about them in other ways and that wasn't right either.   I was the adult. I messed up. Left myself vulnerable. I've paid a price which has been reduced thanks to Karla and the truth coming out. It does not excuse what I did, but what I did was not illegal."

Not wanting to dredge the whole sordid mess up again Jenna said "Just because a girl is a certain age doesn't mean she is fair game or that she should be encouraged by an older person to put herself at risk".

"I can't change what happened. It is in the past. Don't forget Jenna I too have paid a price?"

"What are you wanting from me Curtis?"

"I want to know that if I see you on the street you will speak to me even though that is unlikely now. I am going to be living quite a distance from here. I want to know that there is peace or at least a truce between us before I go. I want you to know that I never intended for you or your family to be hurt by what happened."

"I accepted all that when Karla spoke to me at Christmas. Curtis did you ever think that if you had come and told me in the first place what was happening it may never have got to this point?"

"Yes but I didn't want to damage our friendship."

"Life can be so ironic can't it. You didn't damage our friendship you destroyed it. Take care Curtis."

"And you too Jenna." And with that Curtis walked down the steps with a spring in his step got into his vehicle and drove away from Jenna.

Jenna watched and felt a weight lift from her. Things would never be the same between them ever again, and neither would they as people be the same again, but there was calm, peace and respect restored once again.

CHAPTER 21

Jenna sat in her new home feeling dwarfed by the furniture surrounding her, in spite of her having had a massive clear out of things she knew were of no real use to her anymore.

Over the Christmas break Jenna had given all the children an opportunity to go through and retrieve or claim what they wanted to have from their possessions which had been boxed up and stored away for many years.

Likewise prior to Richard and his family leaving for Australia Jenna had given them all the things they had stored at her place to sort through and take with them.

Jenna had surprised herself at her own ruthlessness in clearing clutter and possessions prior to her move, but here she sat pondering the amount she had with her.

This house was much smaller than the last and the storage space, well it was limited to say the least. Limited by Jenna's standards, but by modern standards very generous.

Not being a defeatist, Jenna got a pad and pen and began listing all the things she had left.

Item in Column One: Needed Yes/No and Column Two: Why?

Once Jenna started listing and sorting she found her time that afternoon had slipped by and her growling stomach reminded her dinner time was upon her.

The piece of paper and pen along with the lists in the columns became piles on the floor.

It was as Jenna was rising rather un-ceremoniously from the floor using the arm of the sofa for support that her door-bell rang.

Steadying herself as she rose Jenna headed for the door with one foot quite tingly.

"Jenna how nice to see you, all. Settled in are we?" asked Johnathon her new neighbour from two doors down.

"Not really." Said Jenna a little more

forcefully than she had intended.

"Good, good. Thought I might take a look around. See what you've done with the place."

"You are more than welcome to have a look around Johnathon but not today. I am still unpacking and the place is in quite a state as you can imagine I'm sure."

"Never mind I am quite adept at stepping over things. Not too worry."

Jenna was trying to hold the door steady so as to stop Johnathon from barging in when they both heard a car coming up the driveway.

"Looks like I am not your only visitor." Johnathon said.

"The boys in blue no less. What have you been up to?"

The Police car pulled up and two Police Officers got out.

"Good afternoon. There was a break in next door this afternoon and we were wondering if you heard anything?" The police officer asked Johnathon.

"Not me. I'm afraid I can't help you. I don't live here. It is the lady of the house you need to speak to. Anyway I'm off. Catch up with you later then." Johnathon said beating a hasty retreat.

"Did you hear anything Mrs. Brown?"

"No I didn't and I am not Mrs. Brown

she is no longer with us sadly. I am
Jenna Mitchell. I shifted in yesterday.

"Were you in this afternoon?" one of
the Officers asked.

"Oh yes. I've been sorting out what to
get rid of."

"I do that before I shift." he said
shaking his head.

"As did I, but I daresay my memories
are more extensive than yours and
memories as you will learn young man are
not always easy to get rid of."

"I'm sorry did I offend you?"

"I am tired that's all. What time this
afternoon did the break in occur?"

"Well Mrs. Crawford left to do some
shopping at 1.30pm"

"I see. So no one was at the house
then?"

"No as I said Mrs. Crawford"

Jenna interrupted him with "Left to
do the shopping at 1.30 pm. Yes I don't
have a hearing problem. It's just that I saw
a small truck going along the road and
slowing down as if to turn into a driveway,
and that was shortly before two o'clock."

"Mrs. Mitchell you said you didn't
hear anything."

"That's right" said Jenna "But I did
see a small truck. A white truck. I wrote
the number down because as I said it was

indicating, no wait it had its hazard lights on, and the gears were being graunched, and I thought that was quite odd so I wrote the number down. I will get it for you."

"She couldn't have seen the number plate. A lonely woman trying to be helpful" the police officer said to his colleague.

Jenna came out with the number written on the paper.

"What took you so long? Bit hard to find the paper?"

"No I was writing it down for you as a copy. Even the Police lose things." Said Jenna handing the number plate number over.

"Excuse me Mrs. Mitchell for asking but how could you have seen the number plate from here?" asked the second police officer.

"I didn't. I was at the letter box collecting my mail. Decided to stretch my legs and the truck was, actually now that I think about it, there were three people in the front seat. Quite large people. They were all scrunched up. I took my pen out of my pocket and jotted the number plate down. Neither of you believe me, do you? Just wait here." Jenna instructed and walked back into her house appearing moments later with the envelope and the number plate number written on the back of it.

"Why would you write this down at your letter box?"

"Well I often jot things down. I always have a pen on me and usually a small pad."

"Jenna Mitchell. Are you Jenna Mitchell the writer?"

"Yes I am."

"Mark Denton. My mother has talked about you."

"Look I should have rung the Police but I have just shifted here and I got busy. I am sorry."

"What you have given us is very helpful. Thank you we will be in touch."

And with that comment the two police officers returned to their car and drove away.

Jenna felt awful. She immediately grabbed her jacket from the coat hook and left her house to walk along to her neighbour's house.

Knocking on the door a woman much older than herself answered the door and Jenna promptly introduced herself offering assistance.

"Thank you so much, but I am in a bit of a state. I have been mopping and cleaning up. They took stuff and made an awful mess.”

“Do you have someone you can stay with?”

“No my family are overseas at present and I don’t want to bother anybody. I will be all right. It is very good of you to come.” Said Mrs. Crawford

“Well at least let me help you with the cleanup. Two hands are better than one.”

With the cleanup done, Jenna made sure Mrs. Crawford had her dinner organized before she left.

Phone numbers were exchanged and Jenna had offered to call back in the morning.

Returning to her own house Jenna looked at the muddle and decided it wasn’t such a muddle after all and set about getting her own dinner on the go.

CHAPTER 22

A couple of weeks later Jenna was shopping when she banged into Mrs. Crawford literally.

Jenna was looking at an item on the supermarket shelf and had taken a step back when Mrs. Crawford had come quite quickly around the corner and the two met in the middle so to speak. Both women were a little shaken but laughed it off.

Jenna suggested they go to the local coffee shop and have afternoon tea together.

Mrs. Crawford was sitting by the window with her number clearly displayed and Jenna was still in the queue.

Having placed her order and holding her number Jenna made her way to the table where she joined Mrs. Crawford.

"I am sorry to have kept you waiting."

Jenna said as she sat down.

"You don't have to apologize I could see there was a hold up."

"Yes indeed. The lady in front of me was taking a while to place her order."

"That's Mrs. Bray." Mrs. Crawford told Jenna.

"Well she was burgled yesterday afternoon. She is very upset. She was telling the girl."

"Tracey. The girl. Is her niece."

"Oh I see. They took her jewelry and small items like her crystal bowl and other precious items."

"Mrs. Bray lives not far from us now. She shifted into one of those new homes in the subdivision just down the road from you. About six doors down."

Mrs. Crawford was looking at Jenna as though Jenna was very thick or disengaged.

"Interesting." said Jenna. "You know Mrs. Bray had had a visitor."

"Not the kind you invite into your home that's for sure." replied Mrs. Crawford.

Jenna smiled realizing that they were talking about two different things but possibly the same thing in the wider scheme of things.

Jenna was determined at that very

moment to ring Constable Denton when she returned home.

"How long have you lived at 1082 may I ask?" Jenna asked.

"Not long actually. My son saw a private sale notice one day on his way home from work and we had a look at the place. I needed something a bit smaller but still with some room for when the grandchildren visit. I've been there a couple of months now."

"Yes we all seem to be relatively new."

"You were so lucky the family sold the house to you. It had sat empty for so long, and houses they need to be lived in I believe." Mrs. Crawford stated.

"Yes I quite agree."

"You have quite a bit of space there don't you?"

"Well yes. I know it sounds silly but it seems quite small now I have shifted in. My last place was very big. The place before that smaller than my current place yet I feel quite confined. It is odd isn't it how we become our environment?"

"I hadn't thought of it like that, but yes I do believe you are right. I was raised in England you know. We came here when I was fourteen and do you know I still think like I am in England. I still talk like I did in England even though the accent has diminished over the years. The formative years are so crucial to one."

"Mrs. Crawford can you tell me how you fill your day in?"

"I read and I have to say it is becoming more and more difficult to find a good modern writer who can write without swearing in their books or blow by blow accounts of a sexual nature. I mean I love reading historical dramas, a good crime novel, true story but modern writers seem to". She paused and Jenna added "Write to the times of the day. Their environment?"

"Well yes when you put it like that you are exactly right."

The rest of the afternoon tea went well and Jenna learned that in addition to reading, Mrs. Crawford was quite the green thumb and could grow pretty much anything. Jenna made a mental note to call Mrs. Crawford for any gardening issues.

They parted on a laugh and Mrs. Crawford invited Jenna to her place the following Wednesday morning for a cuppa.

Jenna made her way home and found Johnathon walking around the property.

"I was just looking for you." He said as Jenna got out of her car.

"Johnathon I'm afraid your timing

isn't very good I am just waiting for the Police."

"Really?" He said looking quite confused "You haven't been burgled?"

"I hope not. Look I don't mean to be rude."

"Yes of course. Perhaps another time then." Johnathon said as he made his way down the driveway passing the police car turning into Jenna's driveway.

Jenna was visibly relieved to see the Police car arriving and moved hastily to the front door to unlock it. Turning Jenna waved Constable Denton to come in.

"Good afternoon Mrs. Mitchell."

"Constable Denton come right in don't be shy."

"You asked to see me?"

"Yes I did."

"I received the message on route. So how can I be of help?"

"Actually I may be able to help you." Jenna said to a very surprised looking Constable.

"You see I have done some research and I want to run something by you. I read a lot of material and I always look at the Crime report in the local Courier. I noticed a trend and far from putting me off from shifting to this part of town I just noted in my diary that burglaries were on the increase in this area. You see." Jenna said showing the constable her diary.

"The trend began around fourteen weeks ago after I had arranged to buy this. Now here is the interesting thing. My neighbor two doors down Johnathon and his grandson shifted into their house just fifteen weeks ago. Now Johnathon is always wanting to look through people's houses. He practically barges in and his Grandson is never seen by anyone. The thing is Johnathon has been in every one's home so I thought that perhaps he is casing the houses for his Grandson."

"I don't think getting to know your neighbours is a matter for the neighbours to make allegations of this sort."

"I am not making an allegation I am looking at information and the time of it. There is a pattern you see."

"Mrs. Mitchell this is not one of your books."

"Exactly this is about catching a burglar. I can see you don't believe me but can you at least check Johnathon out or talk to him?"

"I can't promise you anything. The thing is we have fingerprints but we have nothing on file that matches them, which leads me and others to think these are kids taking small items which are easy to sell on."

"Well that is one theory I have another and my gut tells me this man Johnathon is not what he appears to be. He's shifty and I don't like him coming around at all.

CHAPTER 23

Jenna was walking around the municipal gardens enjoying the fragrant roses, while observing families and couples in their own lives doing their unique things, without noticing that they were being observed or caring if the truth was known. They were engaged with their lives and fully engaged in the moment, and Jenna found that to be extremely refreshing.

This was one place where people could go in the town and there were no street cameras, no shops, and no traffic to negotiate. Like a beach you could walk and talk freely. There is an absolute freedom in that Jenna realized.

No hustle and bustle here, just relaxation or quiet contemplation or whatever you wanted really and those days seemed but a distant memory to

Jenna at times.

Jenna watched a young family, mum and dad with three children walking around the gardens with the parents watching as their children went ahead of them. That had been her once a woman. A mother. A person in a marriage. Funny how you can compartmentalize yourself after the dust has settled. When the children were young they were that young family. Once all the children were at school the fabric of their family had changed from silk to linen then over time to what felt like rough sacking.

So gradual the changing of the times that it was hard to notice unless an event occurred and you felt scratched by it in some way.

I wonder where all these people will end up thought Jenna. Will their lives pan out the way they hope. Would they be better? Worse? Does anyone ever really know what they want or where they want to be or end up?

"We are the choices that we make." Jenna's publisher had told her once.

Life reduced to one of its simplest forms said by someone who was in the position to make all her own choices and never at the whim of another person in her life.

That too was one of her choices, having seen her mother abused by her father and others over the years, she had decided to go through life on her own, on her own terms, and she had made a huge success of it.

But when you are part of a unit, a group, a family, your choices do affect others and their choices affect you.

There is an inexplicable intertwining that happens below the surface which is not necessarily visible or obvious. It is the little things, the small compromises, small changes, daily or built on over time. So small are they that they are missed by the very people they affect.

Jenna had an appreciation of this now, and as time passed she could see the ripples that had become giant waves culminating in the betrayals she had suffered.

The boarder entering their home, changing the dynamic of their family. Adam using the distraction to create a path for himself within, and outside of the marriage.

The flow on effects, with Jenna now older, alone, and sitting on a park bench viewing all these occurrences as one would look at a picture through a kaleidoscope. Bits and pieces scattered and fractured through the glass prisms, with a clear picture emerging despite all the odds in the end.

Jenna was part of the bits and pieces and she had long ago accepted that, but when you put it all together by any other circumstances the people in the frame would have ended up in different places, with different people and by default had different lives.

Jenna now retired unexpectedly early thanks to Adam's financial skill, had by her conservative estimation, a good 25 to 30 years left to live.

No family popping in to keep an eye on her, she was looking at a blank canvas which since she had shifted into her new house was still blank.

Jenna resolved while sitting there on that park bench and watching other people engaged in their lives, that she had better start engaging more proactively in her own life.

She would start, she decided by making her new house into her new home and decided on buying a piece of art work of her choice for her lounge.

With this thought in mind Jenna stood up and began her last lap of the gardens before heading home.

Jenna had been home for a good hour

bagging up the last of the things she really didn't need for the opportunity shop, and was making herself a cup of tea when the computer signaled the Skype ring.

Jenna walked over to her computer and answered it. "Hi there, we miss you." Said Steph and the rest of the day with Jenna's contemplations melted away.

The chatter didn't slow between all the parties and they all looked great, sounded great, sounded happy and Jenna told David that the move for them as a family seemed to be the right one for now.

At the conclusion of the call Jenna felt as if a great weight had been lifted from her shoulders. Perhaps without realizing it Jenna had been carrying the burden of worry about their shift, and how she was going to cope without them and here was her answer.

On the very day she had been in reflection they had contacted her and they were fine and Jenna realized in that moment that she too would be fine, and her blank canvas now had a bright breezy hue to it.

For the next two weeks Jenna began in earnest her search for a piece of art for her lounge. She went to shops, galleries, exhibitions, to no avail and decided one Thursday afternoon to drive to the beach.

Jenna had done this drive many times and found it relaxing whether the car was full of people or not.

It was on her way back from the beach that Jenna noticed a small art and craft shop and decided to turn the car around and go back to have a look.

The place looked deserted, but Jenna opened the door gingerly before walking in to the shop.

"Come in don't be shy." A voice said. "You can look and touch in here all things are fixable."

Jenna was trying to find a face to go with the voice when the face popped up from behind the counter.

"Good afternoon and welcome."

"Good afternoon" replied Jenna.

"Is there something in particular you are looking for?"

"Yes I am looking for a piece of art for my lounge."

"Sculpture? Painting?"

"It sounds silly but I am leaning towards a piece of wooden art."

"Stay right there. I have the perfect thing looking for the perfect space. Be right back."

Jenna was quite bemused by this young man. He had enough enthusiasm and where with all to be able to engage anyone on a journey to anywhere.

"Here you are" he said as he presented Jenna with a cowboy hat made entirely of native timber. Kauri to be exact and the hat detailed with carving was exquisite.

Years before Jenna had seen something similar, and at that time did not have the funds to purchase it.

"Where did you get this?"

"I made it. My grandfather taught me to carve in my teens. I got myself in some strife."

"Did your grandfather live up North in a small place?"

"Yes. He used to send his carvings to Kaitaia."

"Kaitaia? I'm sorry it's just that years ago I saw a hat similar to this one and I have always regretted not being able to buy it."

Overwhelmed and tears appearing the young man said "My grandfather was a good teacher. He gave me a trade and a better life path than I was on."

"You have a gift and your grandfather saw that and has helped you develop and realise that gift. I'll take it."

"Really?"

"Yes really!" said Jenna and with that she purchased the Kauri hat for her lounge, a hat that she had loved when she first saw it. Not the exact same hat but a hat that had been carved with as much love as its predecessor.

On arriving home Jenna hung the hat on her wall in the lounge and with that single act she finally felt at home.

CHAPTER 24

The weeks were slipping by and the garden was beginning to change.

Jenna was spending time sweeping up the last of the autumn leaves. She paused and looked across at the paddocks taking in the grass which appeared to be of differing greens. The day was overcast and the grass looked quite dull in parts.

The sudden increase of wind helped to bring Jenna back to the task at hand. Busying herself with the last section of garden for the season Jenna unloaded the wheelbarrow for the last time and picking up the rake then placing it in the wheelbarrow made her way to the garden shed and put everything away. Jenna locked the garden shed then made her way to the house. On her arrival at the back door she heard a car coming towards the house. Jenna quickly made her way along the path at the side of her house and arrived at the front of the house as Constable Denton was alighting his Police car.

"Good afternoon."

"Yes it has been." Said Jenna brightly. "What can I do for you?"

"Not a thing. I do have some news for you though."

"Now Constable I am intrigued."

"I'm sure you are. You see it is about Johnathon. It seems Johnathon and a war buddy have been quite busy in the town, and other towns in the area."

"I see. I was sure."

"It was the grandson. Yes. Well you might like to know it was the grandson who came to us. He found some items. Anyway it will be in the paper. The court case was today. I was wondering if you knew of someone who may be able to take a boarder in until the end of the year."

"Poor boy he must be devastated." Jenna butted in. "I will ask around. When does he have to be out of the house?"

"Three weeks I believe."

"Leave it with me. Shall I contact you or speak to?"

"Matt. If you contact me I will speak

to Matt. He's a good kid and doing well."

"Would he not do better in a flat with people his own age?"

"Let's just say when he was with people his own age he came to our attention, so he is not that comfortable about returning to that environment just yet. His words not mine. That's what's so sad. His grandfather was supposed to be a positive influence on him."

"Well he has been. He has confirmed to Matt that he doesn't want that lifestyle."

With a smile on both their faces Constable Denton drove away and Jenna returned to her back door.

Once inside the house she went straight to the phone.

"Mrs. Crawford I have some news for you and a request."

And with that the boarder had the option of a home and Constable Denton arrived back at the station with a note to advise him of the same.

Matt shifted along the road to Mrs. Crawford's and proved himself to be excellent company and a good hand at fixing things. His study progressed smoothly and Mrs. Crawford had someone to care for again.

Jenna on the other hand having found herself at rather a loose end had returned to her writing.

Jenna had decided to write a memoir for her family, and in so doing she found that writing non-fiction was quite a stimulating experience for her.

The winter days were short and the nights quite long. The temperatures were cold and the ground was damp or wet most of the time.

On fine days Jenna would walk into town on the newly completed footpath which made it much safer than walking on the road edge, and was excellent for getting out and about safely.

It was always a surprise to Jenna how many people used the new footpath because from the road it looked as if there were hardly any houses nearby.

The new subdivision was tucked away from site from the main road which explained that, but as Jenna got to know her neighbourhood better she learned that there were multiple houses down long and secluded driveways.

Jenna smiled. New people coming, more things happening, trips to her children and grandchildren.

"Yes." She said out loud "It has all worked out in the end even though the middle was a bit mucky."

Walking more lightly and looking

forward to her future endeavors Jenna got on with the busyness of her day.

ABOUT THE AUTHOR

KAREN PIVOTT is the author of *AIRBAGS AND STARTING OVER and is a published radio scriptwriter with HCJB Beyond the Call with Ron Cline series 2001. Radio Southland 2004 and 2005*. Published play write "Gavin's 21st." 2000 Nelson fringe art festival and literacy specialist. Karen lives in Invercargill New Zealand with her husband. Karen loves educating and inspiring people to improve their lives and the lives of all the people they connect with.